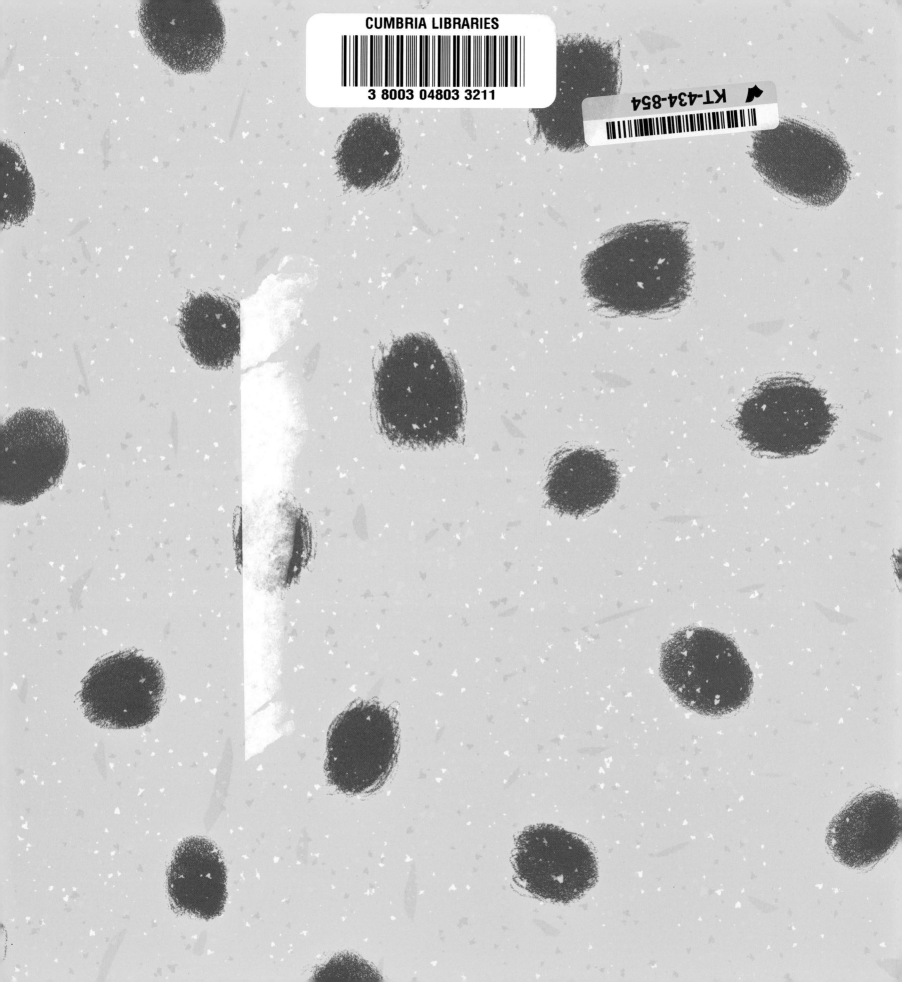

For Dylan Docherty Richards – A.M. For my boys, Charlie and Sam xx – N.R.

First published in Great Britain in 2016 by Andersen Press Ltd.,

20 Vauxhall Bridge Road, London, SW1V 2SA

Text copyright © Angela McAllister, 2016

Illustration copyright © Nathan Reed, 2016

The rights of Angela McAllister and Nathan Reed to be identified as the author

and illustrator of this work have been asserted by them in accordance with

the copyright, designs and patents act, 1988.

First edition.

Printed and bound in China

British Library cataloguing in publication data available.

ISBN 978-1-78344-418-2

SAMSON
the Mighty Flea!

ANGELA McALLISTER

NATHAN REED

ANDERSEN PRESS

Samson was the big star
of Fleabag's Circus.
He could lift a match.
He could lift a pea.
He could lift the lovely Amelie.
(And would you believe, he could lift all three!)

"HURRAH!" cheered the crowd. "HURRAH!"

SAMSON the MIGHTY FLEA!

"I am a big star!" said Samson the Mighty Flea.

But Samson wasn't happy.
Though he boasted, full of pride,
he had an empty place inside.

"I need more people to
amaze," he told Amelie.
"It's time to show the
world how strong I am.
Fleabag's Circus just isn't
big enough for me."

Amelie packed Samson's suitcase.

No one saw that she tucked in something small.

No one saw her tiny teardrop fall.

Samson said goodbye to
Fleabag's Circus.

"So long, my friends.
I'm going to be the biggest
star in the world!"

And off he went.

The world was much,
much, much bigger
than Fleabag's Circus.

Samson put up his sign and started performing amazing feats of strength.

SAMSON
the
MIGHTY FLEA!

He lifted a button.

He lifted a stick.

He lifted a stick
more than twice
as thick.

But nobody noticed his thick stick trick.

Samson didn't give up.
He trained day and night.
He made his act more difficult,
more daring, more
stop-and-staring.

"Nobody will notice a flea with a pea," said a beetle.
"Go back where you belong," said a bug.

But Samson was sure he wouldn't be happy
until he was the biggest star in the world.

As he packed up his act he spotted his chance.
"The Circus of Dreams! That's the place to
find a HUGE audience," he thought.
So off he went.

Samson climbed high, where everyone could see him.

He showed off his mighty muscles and super strength.
It was the most awesome performance of his life!
Then he took a bow...

... and the HUGE crowd cheered!

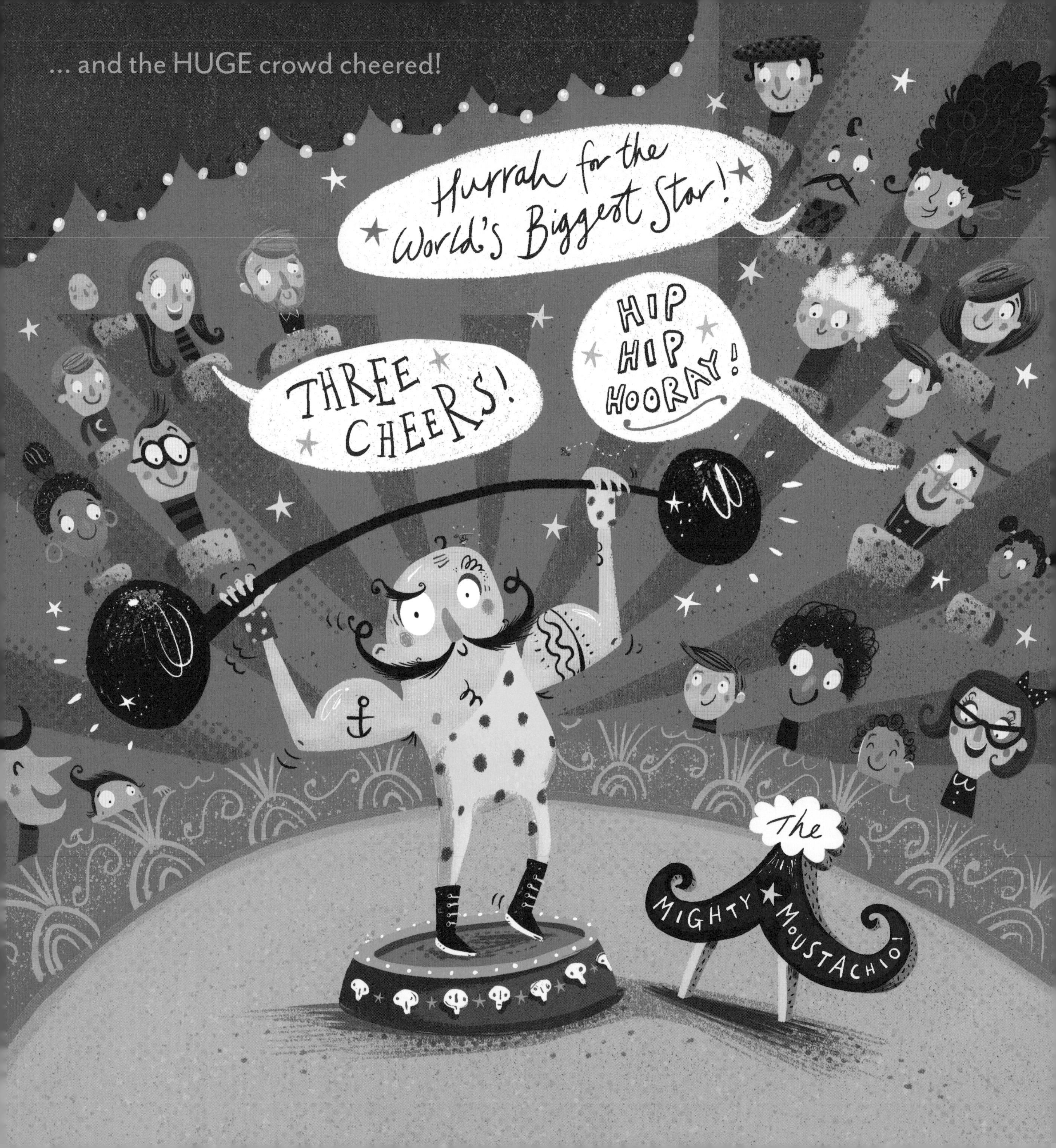

"I'm the biggest star – they're clapping me!"
thought Samson the Mighty Flea.

But something was wrong.
Although he was almost bursting with pride,
he still had an empty feeling inside.
"Cheer up," said a fly. "It's always
lonely at the top."

Suddenly he missed his old friends.
The world seemed very, very far
from Fleabag's Circus.

He left his match. He left his pea.
He left his sign for no-one to see,
and crept off to hide, as sad as could be.

Whoops! Samson's hiding place
started to bounce and shake.

"Hold on tight," chuckled an old flea. "Life's a bumpy journey!"

Samson held on tight, but the
hidden present flew out of his suitcase:
a hankie, stitched with love!

Then he heard
a familiar voice...

You are my
BIGGEST
STAR
Amelie xx

Samson crept closer. Could it be?
Amelie, *his* Amelie, trying to lift a pea?
She swayed... she wobbled...
the crowd jeered, "Boo!"

"You can do it!" cried Samson.
He saw it was true.

She didn't give up.
She raised her brave chin,
she lifted her arms,
so small, so thin...

One, two, three – she did it!

"HURRAH!"
cheered the crowd.
"HURRAH!"

Samson gazed, so proud, so amazed.
So amazed, he felt dizzy and dazed.

He forgot about being big or small,
he forgot about himself at all –
Amelie filled him with happiness.

"Welcome home, Samson," said his old friends.
"Are you the biggest star in the world?"

Samson smiled.
"Fleabag's Circus is the
world for me," he said.

"And its biggest star shines here, for all to see:
the bravest, strongest, loveliest Amelie."

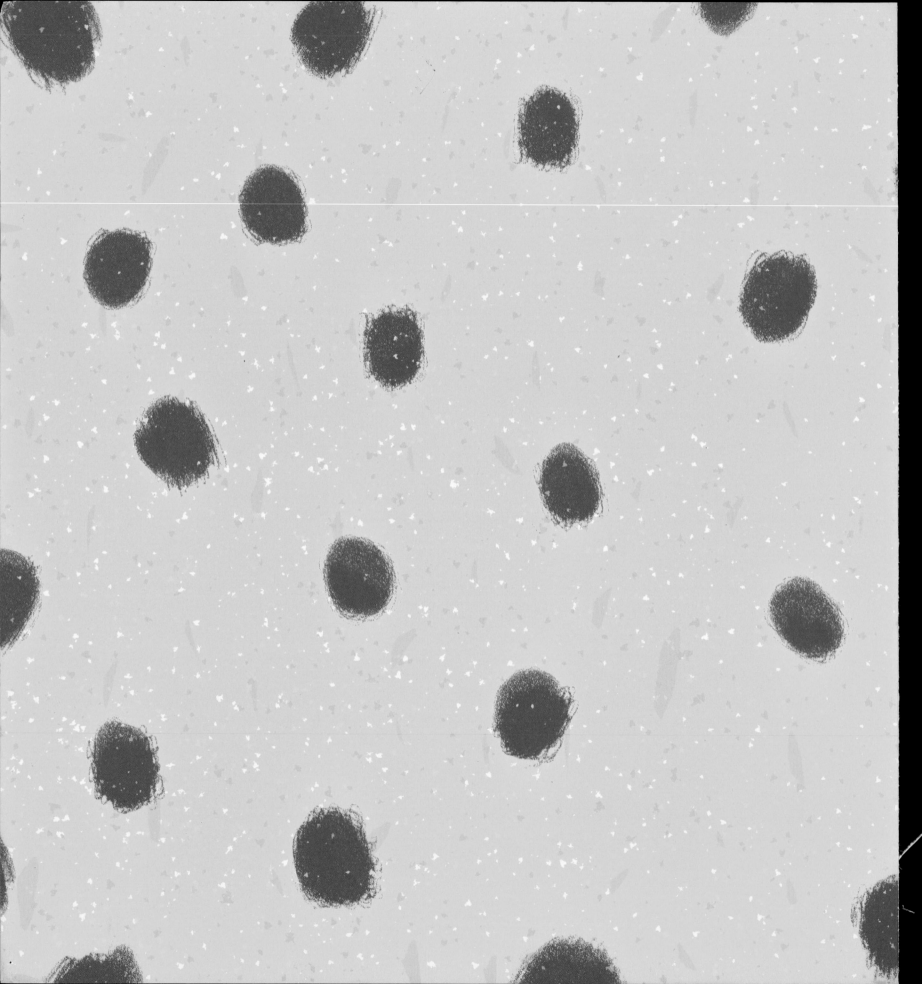